Farmyard Tales

The New Pony

Heather Amery

Adapted by Rob Lloyd Jones

Illustrated by Stephen Cartwright

Reading consultant: Alison Kelly

Find the duck on every double page.

This story is about Apple Tree Farm,

Poppy,   Sam,

Mr. Boot, Mrs. Boot,

Mr. Stone

and a pony.

One morning, Sam,
Poppy and Mr. Boot
went for a walk.

They saw a pony.
"That's Mr. Stone's
pony," said Mr. Boot.

The pony looked sad.
"Poor thing," said Sam.

Poppy fed her
some grass.

The next day, Poppy
returned with a bag
of apples.

The pony gobbled them all up.

The day after that,
Sam came too. But the
pony was gone.

They went into the field to look.

"There she is,"
called Sam.

The pony was caught
on a fence.

They rushed back to
Apple Tree Farm.

Mr. Boot knew what to do. Soon, the pony was free.

That's better.

Just then, they heard a shout. It was Mr. Stone.

He was angry.

"We were only trying
to help," said Poppy.

"Come on,"
said Mr. Boot.

The next morning,
there was a surprise for
Poppy and Sam.

It was the pony!
She was a present
from Mr. Stone.

"He was sorry he was
angry," said Mr. Boot.

20

"Welcome to Apple Tree Farm," said Poppy.

PUZZLES

Puzzle 1

Put the five pictures in order.

A.

B.

C.

D.

E.

Puzzle 2

Fill in the missing word.

gone   shout   pony   sad

A.  They saw a ____.

B.  The pony looked ___.

C.  The pony was ____.

D. Just then, they heard a _____

Puzzle 3

Can you spot the differences between these two pictures? There are six to find.

Puzzle 4

Choose the right sentence for each picture.

A.

They saw a cow.
They saw a pony.

B.

"Can you see her?"
"I can see her."

C.

The pony was gone.
The pony was still there.

D.

Mr. Stone was happy.
Mr. Stone was angry.

Answers to puzzles
Puzzle 1

1C.
2B.

3A.
4E.

5D.

Puzzle 2

A.  They saw a <u>pony</u>.

B.  The pony looked <u>sad</u>.

C.  The pony was <u>gone</u>.

D.  Just then, they heard a <u>shout</u>.

Puzzle 3

Puzzle 4

A. They saw a pony.

B. "Can you see her?"

C. The pony was gone.

D. Mr. Stone was angry.

Designed by Laura Nelson
Series editor: Lesley Sims
Series designer: Russell Punter
Digital manipulation by John Russell

This edition first published in 2016 by Usborne Publishing Ltd.,
Usborne House, 83-85 Saffron Hill, London EC1N 8RT, England.
www.usborne.com Copyright © 2016, 1992 Usborne Publishing Ltd.

USBORNE FIRST READING
Level Two

Farmyard Tales — Pig Gets Stuck

Farmyard Tales — The Runaway Tractor

Farmyard Tales — The Naughty Sheep

Farmyard Tales — Tractor in Trouble

Farmyard Tales — Scarecrow's Secret

Farmyard Tales — Woolly Stops the Train

Farmyard Tales — Pig Gets Lost

The Baobab Tree

There Was A Crooked Man